MARIANTHE'S STORY

TWO

Spoken Memories

ALIKI

GREENWILLOW BOOKS, NEW YORK

Remembering my parents,
all they left behind,
and all they brought forth

Copyright © 1998 by Aliki Brandenberg. All rights reserved. No part of this book may be reproduced or utilized in any form or by any means, electronic or mechanical, including photocopying, recording, or by any information storage and retrieval system, without permission in writing from the Publisher, Greenwillow Books, a division of William Morrow & Company, Inc., 1350 Avenue of the Americas, New York, NY 10019. www.williammorrow.com   Printed in Singapore by Tien Wah Press.   First Edition 10   9   8   7   6   5   4   3   2   1
Colored pencils and crayons were used to create the full-color art. The text type is Korinna BT.
Library of Congress Cataloging-in-Publication Data: Aliki.   [Marianthe's story: painted words]   Marianthe's story: painted words ; Marianthe's story: spoken memories / by Aliki.   p.   cm.
Summary: Two separate stories in one book, the first telling of Mari's starting school in a new land, and the second describing village life in her country before she and her family left in search of a better life.   ISBN 0-688-15661-4 (trade).
ISBN 0-688-15662-2 (lib. bdg.)   [1. Schools—Fiction.   2. Storytelling—Fiction.]   I. Title: Marianthe's story: spoken memories.   PZ7.A397Mar   1998   [Fic]—dc21   97-34653   CIP   AC

In Mr. Petrie's class, everyone was still.
It was Life-Story Time, when the students
had a chance to tell about themselves
so the class could know them better.
Today was Mari's turn.

There was a road that led to our house.
In summer it was dusty and dry as a beetle.
When the cold rains came, it flooded,
and our feet sank in the clay mud.
But when I was born, you could hardly see
the path for the wildflowers,
and the air smelled sweet.

Mama and Papa said it was the happiest day of their lives.
Grandparents, uncles, aunts, cousins, friends—
they all dropped what they were doing.
They tracked up the path to see me.
They pinned good-luck charms on me
and brought fresh honey and bread.
"Long Life! Happy Life!" they said again and again.

The people in our village were so close,
they shared the good and the bad like a family.
During the war, they had mourned together
when so many people were killed—
even people from our village.

They had cried together when my baby brother died
in the famine, before I was born.
The famine had touched everyone.
That is why they were happy to celebrate me.

Mama and Papa celebrated everything—
my first smile, my first tooth, my first steps.
Cousins took me on rides up and down the road.

Yanni brought me figs from his tree.
Nona stood me on the table in front of everyone
to sing the songs she taught me.

Later, when they noticed I was always drawing,
Theo brought me paper from the city where he worked.
He brought news, too, and sometimes even newspapers,
though not everyone could read them.
The nearest school was two long hours away,
and not everyone went.

Life was hard, but people tried not to notice.
"That is what you do when you are alive,"
Mama said. "You work."
We hauled water from the spring.
We scrubbed and cooked and shared the chores.
We made cheese and bread for each other,
and helped to plow the fields and harvest the crops.

At night, under the stars, we rested.
We laughed and gossiped and told stories.
The others even listened to mine.
We'd hear a crunch in the shadows,
and someone would say,
"Here comes Yanni," or "Welcome, Nona."
We recognized each other's footsteps.
That's how close we were.

Then something wonderful happened.
Our twins were born—
boys who looked just like the baby we had lost.
Mama and Papa cried from happiness,
and we all celebrated.
But now there was more work to do than ever.

People were leaving our poor village.
They were going to a new land,
hoping for a better life.
First the fathers left, to work and save
until their families could join them.
We heard that in the new land
there were schools around every corner
and libraries full of books.
That is what Mama and Papa wanted for us.
That is why Papa decided to go, too.

When Papa left, it hurt.
We missed him so much, I drew pictures about it.
Mama said we must be patient and brave.
"He is alone, but we have each other."

Theo was like a papa.
His visits cheered us more than the magic
he pulled out of his bag.
"Pencils and paper for my artist," he said.
"A ball for the twins,
and sweet soap for my sweet sister."
"Mmm, sweeter than the soap we make," Mama said.
He read us Papa's letters about the new country,
his hard life, and how he missed us.

At last I started at the school far away.
Not everyone approved.
"She is only a girl," some said.
"Girls don't need books to clean the house."
"Girls need books to find other worlds,
just like boys," said Mama.
"You will look and listen and learn," Mama told me.
"Someday you will be happy you did."
"I'm happy already," I said.

Every morning before daybreak,
our little band of students
set off down the dark road,
and I sang all the way.

I learned to write letters, then words.
Soon I could recognize them in my book.
Mama was so proud when I wrote my first letter to Papa,
and he wrote back that he couldn't believe his eyes.
It made time go faster, to write and draw
what we were doing in the village.

And then the day came—the day of our sad good-byes.
Good-bye to the people and the village we loved.
Good-bye to all the things we knew—
the trees, the rocks, the birds.
We set off with our bags on the long journey
to the land far away, where Papa was waiting.

The room was quiet when Mari finished,
and she was also still.
"Well, Mari," said Mr. Petrie, "we were waiting for you, too,
and nobody knew it. Welcome to your new life."